Black Water

Barbara Henderson

pokey

First published in 2019 by Pokey Hat

Pokey Hat is an imprint of Cranachan Publishing Limited

Copyright © Barbara Henderson 2019

ISBN: 978-1-911279-62-4
eISBN: 978-1-911279-63-1

Interior Illustrations © Sandra McGowan

Extracts from Riding Officer's Crawfurd's Journal, February 1792
Dumfries Collection: Dumfries District
Source: NLS: Walter Scott papers MS910f49

Cover Illustration: Sail Illustration
© canstockphoto / basel101658

For Rob,
the undisputed King of the
'Address to the Haggis'

'A glittering, real-life adventure swirling with secrets, suspense and nail-biting action.'

Ally Sherrick

Author of *Black Powder*
&
The Buried Crown

Note to the reader:
This story is based on real events
& historical records

Contents

1. Solway Seas   1
2. Crawford's Mission   8
3. Musketry   21
4. The Poet   29
5. A Great Deal of Trouble   40
6. With Pistol & Sword   48
7. Of Quill & Ink   56

Glossary   64
Author's Note   66
Smuggling in Scotland   69
Historical Extracts   71
The Poems of Robert Burns   75
Acknowledgements   79
About the Author   81

1

Solway Seas

Early hours, 28th February 1792

The boat drifts. I try to sit as still as possible, so Father doesn't beat me. He said he would—if I fail him.

A thin layer of black water swills back and forth around my feet and I wish I had taken off my boots, but it's too late now. Father is standing up as straight as he dares, I suspect. If I close my eyes for a moment, the night can't get any blacker and there is a joy in that. I squeeze my lids shut so hard it hurts: something I can control. Unlike the many things I can't. Whether anyone is caught and our mission succeeds. Whether Old Finlay keeps his word.

And whether the boat holds together, and we live or die.

'Sir...' I begin, but it only earns me a clip round the head and a "*Wheesht!*"

I sense my father more than I see him, towering, balancing, straining for land. The darkness is dense, and waves lick the side of our boat, stealing a taste before the meal. I swallow.

'Henry! There!'

If he's pointing, I can't see a thing. *Oh, there, yes.* A light, swinging up and down, there on the coast. Old Finlay's signal.

'Go on, boy! Row!' Father throws his weight onto the bench beside me and what seems like a pailful of black salty water sweeps in.

'Keep still, boy! No-one must hear.'

I take the strain of the oars and press my lips together so hard that I taste salt and blood. *Not a sound, Henry. Not a groan, not a gasp; nothing must give us away.*

The faraway cry of a shearwater and the gentle lapping of the waves are both drowned out by the blood rushing in my ears. Finlay's light disappears for a minute or so, but then it reappears and we have to adjust our course a little. Father, just a crouching shadow beside me, hisses a bad word, but the wind carries it out to sea.

Then the signal: a tap on the shoulder and I lower the oar slowly into its hook. We drift. The faraway hulk of Criffel skulks in and out of the moonlight and I fancy I hear the rocks of the seabed grind beneath us. It must be shallow.

I squint to see Old Finlay's light again, beckoning the smugglers and their boat to shore. All the while, Father is looking across the water—and then I hear them too. Beside me, I can feel my father's hairy hand creep towards his Flintlock pistol.

Voices, strange and urgent. On the water like us, but a small distance away and brazen, with no attempt to keep quiet.

'Gie us that light again, Finlay. She's low in the wa'er tonight,' one of them shouts.

'Aye. Tha's better,' the other hollers a second later.

Old Finlay on the beach stays silent, as he promised.

Two voices: one hoarse and one deep, both with a strange twang like Manx or even Irish. Not that I really think about them, with my tight-wound father beside me and a deadly weapon in his hand. Without a sound, he places his finger on my mouth before reaching down— soundlessly closing his free hand around the rope. He raises the gun.

Suddenly, our boat is jolted by an unexpected impact: we've run aground. From then on, everything happens lightning-fast. Father's Flintlock goes off in his hand and a loud shot rents the black night sky. Startled cries ring out from all, especially me, and it gives away our position. Father aims the gun across at them once more.

Over by the shore, Old Finlay must have dropped his lantern onto the rocks, for there is a loud clang and what little light there was disappears. Footsteps—*is he running?* It's hard to imagine someone with such a white beard run anywhere at all, but I'll be bound he'll be halfway back to his hut by the time we are done here.

The old man may have tipped us off about the boat landing tonight, but he won't want those men to know it.

And only then do I realise what Father is going to do, with his raised pistol, in his fervour not to let the villains escape. Something he could hang for. *Let him beat me, if that's what it takes!*

'No!' I throw myself over towards his gun arm, forcing it down. The shot is deafening: a splash and a thud and a splinter and a cry, all together, here in the Carsethorn shallows. But I've misjudged my distance, and tumble right over Father's side of the boat, teetering for a second or so before losing my battle with gravity. The cold, black water swallows me. Father's voice is muffled, as if from another world. There is another shot, or several, but all is drowned in the darkness.

'Henry!'

It's not deep—I feel the shifting pebbles beneath my boots, but my lungs are full of burning brine and I don't know which way is up or down. My leather jerkin sinks like a dead weight and I struggle, struggle.

'Heenryy!'

Flailing, I hear my name from afar, as if a whole ocean separated me from the caller. But then a strong hand grabs me by the collar and drags me onto the stony beach. I turn onto my stomach and allow myself to heave, but Father thrashes straight back into the sea, his high leather boots shining in the intermittent moonlight. His gun is held high above his head to keep it dry, and the rope is tied around his waist.

'I, John Lewars, Exciseman, hereby arrest you for smuggling contraband wares. I order you to come ashore at once. AT ONCE! I have reinforcements. You are surrounded.'

There is squelching and vile cursing, but soon, two bedraggled men stand before Father and he points the gun to each of their heads in turn. 'Henry! Tie them up!'

I stagger to my feet, but Father taught me well. The knot will hold, no doubt whatever about that. The horizon over the hill is lightening, ever so gradually.

'Surrounded ye say? By you and this… *boy*?' The ruffians exchange a glance.

Father seems satisfied. 'Henry, the evidence—bring the evidence ashore.'

'With respect, sir… what…?'

'In the name of goodness, Henry! Use your brain! The Good Lord gave you one, did he not?'

My cheeks burn, but the rest of me shakes as I collect the wares now washing up on the shore: several large tins of salt, six canisters of tea and two fives of wine. Their boat has all but disappeared: it seems I made Father shoot a hole in its side.

He speaks quietly. 'You may yet make an Exciseman, Henry. One day.' His brief smile banishes the shiver and the darkness.

Because my father's pleasure is all I need.

2

Crawford's Mission

Morning, 28th February

We arrive home as the sun rises over the distant hills out east, and Father barely speaks, his boots still heavy with damp. Mother is already up and is setting out a brew for us. 'There is an urgent message from that Mr Crawford on the table, John. How did the boy do?' she asks before she looks at me at all.

'Tolerably well,' Father grumbles, and ruffles my hair. I stay rooted to the place, hoping the feeling will linger a little longer—his approval is rare and has to be savoured when it comes. My dominie used to say that the Lord had made my head for words, not numbers, before I left the school to learn the Excise trade. I wish one could stay at school beyond thirteen; I liked words, even the Latin ones, and the stories. One doesn't hear many stories in the Excise. Dull numbers, for the most part.

I struggle to unlace my own boots, crusted as they are with salt and seaweed and whatever else. There is still the reek of contraband. I don't see the appeal of the alcohol—the stench is so very foul. I wonder that any man of sound mind should wish to pour it down his own throat!

'Shall you take him again soon?' Mother continues, narrowing her eyes and noticing the shiver I just gave as my cloak squelches to the floor. But Father doesn't answer. He is reading his message from the new Riding Officer, Mr Walter Crawford. It can't be a good one: his forehead furrows in the dim light of the house.

There is a pause before he answers. 'You mean Henry? Yes, I shall—though he has much to learn. We are dealing with men of depravity, so much is clear. No god-fearing Scot would evade justice like the people of these shores. Look!'

He holds up the paper to show Mother, but

the little one has begun to cry and Mother does not know her letters well in any case. Father clears his throat and reads it aloud:

'*Reports of a large smuggling vessel, just entered the Solway Firth, have reached me. It was spotted near Annan and we suspect that it is manned by armed rascals. Naturally, I have sent for protection. A group of Dragoons are on their way, and I beg your assistance at the earliest opportunity. Yours etc ...*'

He sighs deeply. Annie, our second youngest, toddles by and he absent-mindedly follows her with his eyes before turning to Mother. 'Jean, I'll require bread and cheese this instant! And dry clothes too.' He gestures at me. 'Henry, make haste. We need fresh horses before we ride east to Annan. Make haste, make haste!'

My mother hurries to the dresser to fetch plates. I scrub the salt off my skin with cold water and bone soap, rubbing myself dry so hard that my skin feels raw, and button my second-best pair of breeches. I'll fetch the horses, *I certainly shall. But not before paying a secret visit to Old Finlay.*

He may know things.

If only my pony wasn't so tired from last night, and so stubborn to boot! My entrance is considerably less impressive than I would have hoped, trying to trot down the lane while it keeps lowering its head to snatch a clump of grass.

'Finlay.'

Silence.

'Finlay, open the door.' I whisper it now, like I do at night when Father sends me with his messages, but I'm not sure the old man hears me. I can't see anyone around, so I risk it and knock louder. The old man's donkey brays in the field, as if to announce my arrival to the world.

'Finlay. It's Henry Lewars. Open the door.'

I press my ear against the weathered wood and fancy I feel the chill seep right into me through it. There is a little stirring, a twitching at the plain cloth that serves as a curtain for the window beside the door, and then a clang, as if something was knocked over in a hurry.

The door opens a chink.

'Please go away. Granda's nae well,' says Finlay's

granddaughter, Mary. She is a little younger than me, and already in service as a kitchen maid in one of the big houses, but she does look in on the old scoundrel from time to time. *This will complicate things.*

'Let me through. I come on the order of Riding Officer Crawford.'

She tries to bar my way, but I push past her.

It takes a moment for my eyes to adjust to the dark of the smoky house. The old man's face looks even more wrinkled than usual, and he is wearing a night gown although the sun is high in the sky. I feel a pang of jealousy and the sudden urge to yawn.

'Begone, Mary. I have need of speaking with your grandfather alone.'

'You're a lad, that's a'—just like I'm a lass!' Her eyes are defiant. 'I'll stay. Dinnae distress him, d'ye hear?'

'M-Master Henry,' Finlay stutters. 'Whit's wrang? Whit's happened?'

'Finlay, there is word of a schooner in the Firth. Not just a boat—*a schooner*! Aren't you surprised?'

I watch the old man narrowly. Only a few years ago, he was arrested while rowing contraband salt across the Solway himself. Why, oh, why do these people risk so much for a tin of salt, or some candles, or brandy, or whatever it is!

The message is clear: pay the proper taxes on what you need, or do without these things. It's simple—is it not? In any case, Old Finlay was poor then and couldn't pay his fine. Father let it pass, but only in exchange for information. Now the old man helps our officers by telling them what he overhears, but I wouldn't be surprised if he withheld as much as he offered. Finlay still is a poor man. He'll side with whoever pays, regardless of the law. I scrutinise his face.

There is a momentary darting aside of the eyes, a shifting of the step, which is all the confirmation I need.

'Finlay. You knew. You KNEW?'

I wonder at how a thirteen-year-old son of the Excise can make a poor lame fisherman quake so. He doesn't know what to say, or what to do. I place my hands on my hips.

'Finlay, you guided us to that small boat, miles

along the coast in the opposite direction, when all the while there was a schooner heading east? Was this a diversion? By design?'

He blanches. 'Naw, Master Henry, dinnae, please dinnae …'

'Tell Mr Lewars, you mean? Have no doubt: my father *will* certainly hear of this if you don't divulge everything now. Where is this schooner headed? Who is involved? What's it carrying? Finlay, look at me!'

'I said, dinnae distress him!' Mary copies my stance and glares at me, but I ignore her. The old man has sunk to his knees in his night gown and my heart stirs a little. He has fewer choices than I… or anyone of my station in life. For a dark, smoky moment, compassion gets the better of me.

I drop the anger from my voice. 'Very well. My father won't hear of your trickery but tell me. Is it true?'

He hesitates, shuffles to the window and pulls the cloth aside a chink.

'Look, there is no-one here to eavesdrop. Speak freely, old man!' My words sound steely now; I am running out of patience.

He takes a deep breath and exhales very slowly, as if weighing up his words.

'There's a schooner right enough, a large vessel from doon south. It is carryin' weapons from Guernsey, and a' manner o' things from Europe. Wine, spirits, tea, tobacco. But oh, it's an armed vessel, Master Henry. The sailors arenae from these parts. I wouldnae like tae see ye harmed by suchlike.'

'Where is this ship heading?'

His face is a mask of misery. 'She's bound fer Annan, last I heard. Oh, dinnae gae after 'em; I know ye'll come off worse! She's travelling doon the deep channel o' the Solway, where the current is strongest. The beaches are dangerous out that way.'

'No doubt my father will know what to do. Finlay, I won't tell of your deception, but you must promise not to breathe a word of my visit to anyone. To anyone, do you hear?'

I remember Mary. 'Both of you!'

Mary nods, but glares away, her face alive with rage. I know she despises me, but it's of little consequence.

Finlay rises. 'Why would I tell a livin' soul? If anybody knew I was helpin' the Excise, they'd burn the very roof o'er my heid.'

'And if my father knew you're still helping the smugglers, he might do the same!' I give my voice as much authority as I can muster. 'This needs to be the end of your double-dealing, Finlay. You are an informer to the service of the law. And that is the end of it.'

The old man says nothing. He doesn't want to make a promise he cannot keep.

I decide to leave it. I look seriously into his eyes before swinging myself back into the pony's saddle and kicking my heels so it breaks into an outraged trot. I manage to shout over my shoulder, although whether the wind carries my voice away before the old man can hear it, I do not know. 'Mind my words, Finlay, if you value your life.'

At this, the stubborn pony finally begins to canter and I breathe the cold air deeply. I'll need all my wits about me today.

The journey back takes a while, as I have to wait for the new horses to be tacked and saddled at the stables near the Excise Office. They trot effortlessly beside my tired beast. When I arrive home with them all, Father steps out of the house, washed, shaven and no doubt fed. My own stomach rumbles.

'Henry, we've not a minute to lose. There's word from Crawford again. We're meeting him at Annan as soon as we can get there. This will be a proper experience for you—a smuggling operation worth intercepting. Just as well we were back in time, or we may have missed the biggest haul of the year, all for a small boat. I wonder where they're planning to bring the ship ashore.'

'Aren't there plenty of options near Annan itself?'

Father doesn't even question the certainty in my voice. I must be careful.

He strokes his beard. 'Likely. There's sheltered water there, and if all goes wrong, they could head off towards England. Hmm.'

I hand the reins of the pony to wee Frederick,

even though he is only ten. He'll know what to do.

An hour later, I am riding a hired horse, on a grown man's mission. Trust me to end up with the laziest beast again, a tall grey stallion at least twice my age! I have to work hard, and my legs ache as the miles disappear beneath our horses' hooves. The sun is barely past midday when we reach Annan.

'Good afternoon, Crawford.' Father says it as if he had slept last night, as if his attire hadn't been soaked through by seawater only a few hours ago. He nods briefly at the thirteen Dragoons on horseback waiting a little way off.

'Afternoon, Lewars,' says Crawford. He is short and wiry with piercing eyes. 'Brought your son, have you?'

'Henry will observe and learn. He will not be in the way.'

I open my mouth to affirm this before remembering that I must not speak. On no account must I disgrace Father in front of his fellow Excise Officers. I would surely deserve a beating if I did.

'Let's be on our way as soon as your horses have drunk then.' Crawford drums his fingers on his saddle impatiently. 'Just as we sit here idle, the schooner may be unloading elsewhere.' The last comment is directed at me, bent as I am over the trough, allowing my horse to plunge its snout into the clear liquid. The damp of sweat hangs in the air above it, even though it is February.

I swing myself back into the saddle with some difficulty, but no-one seems to notice. The men dig their spurs into their horses' flanks, forcing them into a trot before cantering off, with me struggling to keep up.

We stay close to the coastline, barely speaking. Before long, we turn the headland at Torduff Point and see the ship in the distance. From here it looks magical and otherworldly in the hazy light. I can make out the narrow hull with two masts, large enough for a sizeable crew. Eight or nine sails flutter brightly in the wind, but it's too far away to be sure. I can't help being a little impressed by such a fine vessel.

'She's coming in. We're not too late!' Crawford

shouts without slowing his pace. We are trotting rather than cantering now, and I struggle to sit out my horse's huge strides—riding the pony is so much easier. A stitch has developed in my chest.

Crawford turns in his saddle. 'The ship will hit the sandbanks if it comes in much closer than this. They'll be waiting for the tide and cover of darkness before unloading. *Ha!* We will board her and seize all there is. Forward!'

This is Crawford's mission, and we are here to help him achieve it. I kick the sides of my grey stallion, and reluctantly, he jogs after the men until the daylight is worn-out, just as we are. Behind the schooner in the distance, the sun sets the shallow waters ablaze.

3

Musketry

28th February 1792

The Solway mirrors the sky, framed by an unending sandscape as far as the eye can see.

Mr Crawford pulls his pistol from his lanyard. I glance along—the tide is out and would allow us tolerably close to the ship, I'll wager. *Have the smugglers seen us yet?*

The answer comes in the form of a volley of musket fire, though we are still out of range. I flinch at the shots. It's a warning, make no mistake. Father glances back at me but averts his gaze as soon as I meet his eye. Perhaps he is wondering if it was wise to bring me after all.

'This is what you trained for,' Crawford shouts

to the Dragoons. 'We'll board this ship, and that's all there is to it. Pistols at the ready!'

Mr Crawford swings himself off his horse and when I do the same, he leads his horse over and presses the reins into my hands. 'Your boy can tend to the horses, John,' he says to Father as if I wasn't there at all.

I do as I am told, tying everyone's steeds to the low shrubs by the beach. They all shy and whinny when there is another lot of musket fire from the ship, and one breaks loose in the sudden movement away from the source of the noise. It takes me several minutes to catch hold of it again while the men prepare for their approach.

Father doesn't look back once, and I send a prayer for his safety to heaven, when I'm not distracted by the runaway beast snapping at my hand.

They march down to the beach and out onto the sand-flats. The ship doesn't appear to be moving, but if I narrow my eyes, I can make out figures on deck, running from one end to the other. Our own military, led by Mr Crawford and Father, become smaller, their shapes echoed in the damp sand below them in the February light.

More musketry—I wince—and the men stop, undecided, before proceeding. They are out of earshot now, and I am too occupied with calming the horses in any case.

But then—an almighty boom! There is no mistaking it: smoke rises from the deck of the ship every time the smugglers fire their carronades. *Cannon fire? Here, in the Solway Firth?* The roar of the sea quickly obscures the shouting from our men, but I can see that two of our soldiers have slipped and are being helped up by their companions.

The whinnying and stamping all around me only partially distract me from what I see played out in the distance.

Wild gestures and raised voices draw my eye to our small group; the men are remonstrating with Crawford. Eventually, they edge backwards as another boom rents the air. I am holding four of the horses' reins now, and the others are straining hard against the ties that hold them to the bushes, but it proves to be the last of the hostile fire. Our men are returning, with the cursing Crawford at the front, leaving a trail of deep footprints in the sodden sand.

Back on the verge, Father shakes his head at the ship over his shoulder and the men mutter amongst themselves. But Crawford? He walks right up to the copse of shrubs where I am waiting with the horses. His lips are moving, but silently, as if he is rehearsing a speech of some kind. He reaches up high to pick a straight-ish stick from the tangled mess of branches and wrestles with it until it snaps.

Without a word, he rushes past me and approaches his horse, reaching into a saddlebag and unwrapping a hunk of bread. He is hungry, of course. But no, the bread goes back into the saddlebag, and he unrolls the white cloth which served as a wrapping. Taking a corner of it and a length of twine from his pocket, he fashions himself something akin to a flag. *What is he doing?*

Noticing my confused expression, Father explains. 'Mr Crawford is making a white flag,

Henry. It means surrender; it's a sign that he means no harm. It's…'

He doesn't complete his sentence but spins round to his colleague, stretching both his hands out in an unusual gesture of pleading; beseeching, even. 'Think better of it, man,' he attempts and Quartermaster Manly nods with anxious agreement, but Crawford looks at neither of them.

Instead, he makes for the beach once more. Waving his flag high above his head, he advances, step by squelching step, towards the vessel glistening in the receding waters.

'He's mad,' offers a Dragoon, and earns himself a slap round the ear from his Quartermaster: '*Wheesht!* Mr Crawford is no fool. He is a brave and devoted servant of the state. You, on the other hand, are nobody!' The chastised soldier retreats.

Father has come to stand beside me, and we strain for a better view. I expect the momentary flash of musketry, the bang of a cannon, but the waves and the gulls are the only sounds. Even our horses are calm again, as if a man hadn't just taken his life into his hands, on account of the Excise.

Will that be me? One day? Will anybody ever call me a brave and devoted servant of the state?

I fancy I can feel myself growing half an inch just thinking about it. Maybe there are stories of bravery and gallantry to be had in the Excise service after all.

Father passes constant comment, even though we can see for ourselves what is happening. There are murmurs all around us—passers-by have gathered as word gets around the locals. They all claim to support the government of course, but I wonder what manner of contraband is hidden and stashed all around us, in crevices and moss-holes, dug low into the ground.

There are many ordinary folk who would side with the smugglers, to be sure. No-one in Scotland has taken as enthusiastically to the free-trade as the Solway men, and a sinful curse on the land it is, my grandfather used to say, an Exciseman too. It has always been thus.

Ordinary people resent the heavy taxes on wine, sugar, tea and salt. And why not distil and sell their own whisky without giving the government a share, so they argue. If a bargain is to be had, why pass it up? It should be rightfully theirs. *"They thieve from the state, to live above their station,"* Mother explained when I was very young. It still baffles me that so many men and women are willing to risk the fines.

Father's voice is quiet and hoarse: 'Look, that's Crawford in range now. Definitely in range. They could fire muskets at him and hole him like a sieve, and there wouldn't be a thing we could do… I simply wish he'd turn back. He hasn't got a hope of boarding anyway. Look, he's merely yards away from the hull of the ship—wait—did you see that? Your eyes are better than mine—did something just fall off the side of the schooner? A rope ladder? You're certain?'

The Quartermaster produces a Short telescope from his saddlebag, and my father all but wrestles it from the man, continuing his observations aloud. 'He's climbing the ladder. Oh, is this wise? He is climbing onto the smugglers' ship all by himself. They could hold him hostage, or simply slit his throat.'

His hands rarely stay still, fidgeting and scratching at this and that. I understand: Crawford is new in post, and Father feels responsible for his safety. I squint hard against the light to see if there is any kind of commotion on the boat, but there is no sign of it. Straining my ears, I hear no gunfire either.

Some of the local bystanders are beginning to move on, chatting to each other in low voices, shooting us hostile glances and dispersing east and west with some urgency. I suppose their cattle will still need fed. No sign of Crawford. If Father was restless at the beginning, he is all but unbearable now, snapping at me: 'Henry! Ask for water for the horses at that steading over there!'

I am about to leave when a cry goes up amongst the soldiers.

'There! Look!'

Right enough, someone dressed like Crawford is climbing cumbersomely down the side of the ship.

4

The Poet

28th February 1792

The Riding Officer hobbles over the sandflats, slowly. *Is he hurt?* No, I don't think so. Just weary. Ah no, I see now—he has to be careful—the tide is coming in and the sun has sunk much lower in the sky.

The Dragoons are sitting on the edge of the beach, many having loosened their collars and glancing over to check on Crawford's progress only from time to time. Father, on the other hand, has not taken his eyes off his colleague: 'There's a fair current, once the tide is in properly. Mr Crawford will do well to stay on his feet. People drown in these waters.'

If there was anyone else to debate this with, he would not choose his son. But I *am* here beside him, so he tells me. 'He'll make it back without being cut off, Henry. He will. But only just. *Come on*, Crawford.'

Is it possible that the man in the distance might have heard? In any case, he speeds his steps, with the water reaching as high as his knees. After what feels like an eternity, he splashes to land and we meet him at the water's edge, his teeth chattering. 'Do you have anything I could dry myself with, Lewars?'

Father shakes his head and I make myself useful by running back to the resting military, returning with a saddle blanket and a spare shirt. He and Crawford are already talking tactics with Quartermaster Manly.

'We've no choice but to send for Burns,' declares Crawford. 'I know he is new to the Excise, but he'll want to establish himself.'

'If he doesn't have his head in a book,' the Quartermaster snorts, but Crawford cuts him short.

'Poet or no poet, he's a man of the Excise now.'

The Riding Officer turns to my father. 'Are you one for poetry, John?'

Father's face hasn't quite shed its tension from before. 'I can't say that I am, Mr Crawford. Although I am not averse to a song now and again.' The men laugh, but it's short and business-like.

Crawford rubs his hands. 'That's decided. Fetch Burns and send for reinforcements, fifty soldiers, if they can spare them. And be sure to leave some men here to keep an eye on the ship.'

Father is all out of words. He simply nods to us all—yes, even me—and walks stiffly to where the Quartermaster is talking to his charges. A general commotion ensues as horses are untied, supplies are swapped, hurried messages are written and dispatched to Dumfries and all but six of the soldiers swing themselves into their saddles. Crawford offers a small cask of whisky to the remaining men who express their appreciation loudly.

'Are we going home now, Father?' I venture hopefully while those left behind to guard the ship kindle a driftwood fire and take a dram.

'No, Henry. We are to send for reinforcements from Dumfries while Crawford does the same from Ecclefechan, and then we must stay nearby tonight so we can board the schooner at first light. Mr Crawford is wet through and will catch his death unless we get him to a fireside to dry off. While I write messages, try the farmhouses yonder first. If we have to go to an inn, Gretna is closest.'

It would appear that, no, none of the surrounding farmhouses can offer us shelter for the night, or even a bite to eat. Seemingly, they are all out of hay for our horses too. Mr Crawford is made of sterner stuff than we gave him credit for—far from resting by a fireside, he rides to Ecclefechan to alert more Dragoons—and makes surprise raids on some known smugglers' houses on the way.

But he has found nothing and looks spent. Father's face is also furrowed with fatigue when we finally ride into Gretna that night—deprived of food, of sleep and of success.

By the inn's fireside later, I devour the pie and

ale set before me while Father and Crawford discuss the day's events.

'By all that is sacred, Crawford, how did you entice the ruffians to let you on board?' Father asks as he pours another tankard of ale for the Riding Officer.

Crawford shrugs. 'I came peacefully, to parlay with them. I wasn't sure if they would allow it, but I doubted they would shoot a man with a white flag, for fear of the gallows. The truth is, John, they beckoned me on board to bribe me. To bribe me, yes.' Crawford lowers his voice. 'John, you wouldn't believe the contraband stored on that ship! There was wine, rum, and so many canisters of tea I lost count. Sugar, too— and parcels and parcels of tobacco.'

'How well-defended is she?'

'Well, you all heard the carronades, and there was a good number of men on board, about twenty-four of them, armed with fifteen rounds of shot each. That is a lot of firepower! We will need all the help we can get.'

'And we are unlikely to find it here,' Father growls in a low voice, downing the last of his ale and slamming the tankard down on the table so hard that I jump.

I look over my shoulder. He is probably right. The handful of other drinkers in the room look hostile, averting their gaze as soon as my eyes come to rest on them. I do not understand it— we are servants of the law, employed by the Crown. *Why are we the enemy? Who would side with ruffians when they could side with us?*

There is silence. 'The tide will be in tomorrow morning, so the ship will be afloat,' Crawford says eventually.

'Do you not think that the vessel might drift overnight, on account of the current?' Father asks.

'I hope not. It would complicate things.'

Father gives him a quick, searching look. 'Do you mean…'

'Yes. Quicksand. Those beaches further along are treacherous.'

There is a commotion at the door and all of us turn to see. It is the poet, Robert Burns. I have not made his acquaintance before, though he is handsome, and well known for his verses and songs. Only this month, he began to work for the Excise at Dumfries with Father. If he is nervous on the eve of his first major assignment, he doesn't show it.

'Crawford. Lewars.' He shakes the men's hands warmly before turning to me. 'And young Master Lewars, I presume? Gentlemen, evening all.'

He taps his hat to those drinking at other tables in the inn. They acknowledge him, though that in itself is not surprising, he is famous enough. But then their eyes flit from him to us and come to rest on his gauging stick, used to measure the volume of wine in a cask. The mark of an Exciseman. The faces, friendly and welcoming at first, now shutter inwards to subtle whispers.

'Burns. Take a dram—you've travelled far enough tonight.' Crawford pushes the wooden quaich towards the poet.

Burns smiles easily as he helps himself to the whisky: 'Quartermaster Manly sends word, Mr Crawford. Your reinforcements are on their way. Alongside the six soldiers you have on the shore, there should be forty-four more by tomorrow morn. The Quartermaster will join us at Annan then. Do you expect trouble, sir?'

He addresses Crawford who raises his eyebrows at each of us in turn. 'Trouble? Oh yes. I'll wager there will be a great deal of trouble. In fact, I am sure of it.'

I expected a chuckle, but it doesn't come. Instead, all three men stare ahead into the air in front of them, their mouths set in straight lines. I feel the urge to giggle out of sheer nervousness, but the poet lightens the mood:

'There is no such uncertainty as a sure thing. I'll have another dram, innkeeper, and let's have a song too.'

The innkeeper pours another round. Without accompaniment of any sort, Burns strikes up a song: a brief but cheering tune about a *Gallant Weaver* or somesuch.

> *Where Cart rins rowin to the sea,*
> *By mony a flower and spreading tree,*
> *There lives a lad, the lad for me,*
> *He is a gallant Weaver.*

His voice is pleasant enough, so much so that he earns himself a cheer at the end—even Mr Crawford can't help himself. It is so odd to hear an educated man like the poet use the Scots dialect.

Father seems unimpressed, returning to the topic of our mission: 'Crawford, I was thinking… if you're right about the quicksand…'

'There is no question of riding a horse over quicksand if that's what you are asking. Once the tide comes back in, we simply have to commandeer whatever boats lie nearby and row out to it. Simple.'

At this, several chairs near the window are pushed back and their occupants stamp towards the door and out into the night. The rest of the men in the bar watch us with heightened suspicion.

'You can see it in their eyes,' whispers Burns, a glint of amusement in his. 'They wish the deil awa wi' the Exciseman!'

'I'm going to bed,' says Mr Crawford, abruptly pushing his own seat back.

'Henry, we must retire to our chamber, too,'

Father agrees. 'We'll need to make ready at first light. Goodnight, Burns.'

But the poet is happily humming, sipping from his dram and fetching a graphite pencil from his pocket. He begins scribbling in his notebook, humming a jaunty little tune. I gather my things and make to follow, but something stops me. *What verse can he possibly be writing now? All we have talked about are drams and boats and the Excise. Not the kind of thing one could write a song about, surely?*

I don't know what comes over me, but I stop, mesmerised by the bold scrawl in the poet's notebook. I am a fair reader, and never having seen the Scots words written on the page, my lips form the sounds before I can stop them.

'*The deil cam fiddlin' thro' the town,*
And danc'd awa wi' th' Exciseman.'

The poet blows the graphite dust off the paper and lifts it towards me. 'There's beauty in these words, is there not? I think my ideas are more barren in English than in the Scottish dialect, Master Lewars. Wouldn't you agree?'

My face reddens. 'I am sure I do not know, sir.'

I should have stopped there, but for some reason I add 'I love all words. I love poems and stories and songs.'

He looks at me then, really looks at me. His wink breaks the spell and I run up the stairs to catch up with Father.

It's only when his snoring fills the chamber which we share, that Crawford's words echo in my mind as if they were being spoken into the darkness: *a great deal of trouble. Armed men. Muskets. Carronades.*

The moon is high in the sky by the time I finally fall asleep.

5

A Great Deal of Trouble

Early hours, 29th February 1792

I wake, blinking and thinking. *Is it morning yet?* My bedstead is beneath the tiny window and I risk peeking out past the thick fabric which hangs in front of it, to keep out the light and the cold. It doesn't succeed in either. There was a tiny remnant of a fire in the grate when we arrived, but the innkeeper gave us no more logs, even though we asked. Of course he didn't. We're Excise men.

Dawn and birdsong seep in from the window, and something else too. Whispering.

I sharpen my senses, but it's hard to make out the words.

'Aye, I'm sure. Ma Granda' says it's the whole of the Dumfries Excise, and they've sent for reinforcements, too. He says tae send one o' yer men doon tae the shore, light a signal lantern and then swing it roond three times. That's the signal. It'll tell the free-traders nae tae land any o' their wares here and tae make fer open seas again. Mind, dinnae mention me, or my Granda. He's in enough trouble already. And Granda' says tae tak this for yer troubles. And I thank ye.'

Halt a moment. I know that voice! I sit upright in my bed and press my nose against the condensation of the window, in a desperate attempt to see beyond all reasonable doubt. *What is she doing here?* Old Finlay's granddaughter curtsies briefly to the innkeeper and scurries away to mount the old man's donkey, trotting off towards the Dumfries road, faster than I could get my stubborn stallion to do it. It must have taken her much of the night to get here.

The truth trickles into my brain. *She is warning them!* Getting word to the smugglers that this band of Excisemen does not mean to give up the fight. Telling them to flee.

'Father?' I whisper it tentatively, half-heartedly. I don't want to cause more upheaval, but surely he needs to know?

'Sir!' I try louder. 'I've just heard...'

He stirs a little, fumbles for his pocket-watch on the nightstand and shoots upright. 'My, it's nearly light already! Why didn't you tell me sooner, Henry! Make haste, we are meeting Crawford by the road at first daylight! Down to the stable, Henry, and see that our horses are saddled and ready. And knock on Burns's chamber on the way!'

I obey without question. Father is not often ready to listen—not to Mother, and certainly not to me. I knock at the poet's door, but all I get in response is a drowsy groan. 'Mr Burns, sir—we'll convene by the road.' I do not wait.

Even though we gave strict instructions, none of our horses are saddled and there is no trace of hay in their troughs, but I half-expected that. The stable boy, not much older than me, is particularly sullen and lazy, making every movement at snail speed, despite my many entreaties to make haste, even when I lay out the desperate urgency of the situation. I lose my temper with him in the end, just as I know Father would. Maybe I am more like him than I think.

At long last, our party is ready and gathers outside. Distant tapping and hammering sounds punctuate the dawn chorus. *Who in their right mind would repair their boats at this unholy hour? Strange ways they have, the country folk!*

Crawford appears tense, his hand resting on his pistol more than once as he explains the situation.

'Gentlemen, I have had word that, just as we feared, the ship has drifted further into the Firth with the current. It now lies at Sarkfoot, as near to Gretna as to Annan and it seems that the crew are making every effort to sail her out of the Solway altogether. I cannot think how they would be aware of our plans. After all, they only saw us retreat yesterday.'

Even though Crawford does not, *I* have no doubt how the smugglers knew. Mary!

Crawford continues with grim features. 'In any case, you can be sure of one thing: just as we make ready to confront the smugglers, the smugglers will be making ready to meet us, if they can't succeed in getting away.

'Considering the vast penalties, I can only surmise that they will use their weapons to land and hide everything safely. We will try to ride up to the ship through the shallows. Failing that, we'll lay claim to any boat nearby, if the tide has come in too far to go on horseback.

Crawford continues, 'One thing is clear: they have stranded the vessel for now. There it lies for want of water—I thank God for the bright moon last night, so these observations could be made.'

'How do you propose we board the ship?' the poet asks, looking alert and keen to prove himself, just as Father said he would be.

Mr Crawford clears his throat. 'I suggest approaching the schooner from three different angles: one led by you, Mr Burns; one by me and John here; and one by Quartermaster Manly. With a goodly number of men each, we should have the advantage.'

Father nods. 'That's the way to do it, I concur, Mr Crawford.'

'Aye!' The poet's eyes sparkle, and he smiles at me.

Father seems to remember I am there and turns to me, just to check that I've understood, so I add my own 'Yes, sir.'

Ten minutes later we're on the road, our horses' steps a little weary. Not that it makes much of a change with my stallion, who throws down his neck to snatch a mouthful of grass whenever I slacken the reins. At a burn, all our beasts drink deeply. *Those people at the inn—all scoundrels and smuggler-pawns! They can't have fed or watered our steeds at all!*

Some soldiers join us as we pass yesterday's camp and we trot another mile down the road. There we line up and face the estuary. The schooner is listing badly, unbalanced and leaning left. The sandbank beneath it is visible to the naked eye in the low tide. Crawford's face shines with satisfaction—until the schooner's carronades fire once each. A reminder. And a warning.

Father narrows his eyes. 'Can we ride out to it?'

He urges his horse forward, but Quartermaster

Manly holds him back: 'What are you doing? That's quicksand down there—it's too dangerous!'

'Ah, how bad can it be?' Father scoffs.

'John...' begins Crawford, but Father spins round to him: 'Listen, Walter—I've not had a proper rest in days, and one thing's sure—I'm not going to *get* a rest until that vessel right there on the surf is intercepted. The tide is on the up—what if she slips away? We simply must board her, and there's no time to lose: the angle she's lying at is fortunate for now. Even if they fire, they'll not get a clear shot at us; it's too tight while she's listing like that. We've got to seize her now.'

With that, he urges his mare forward and onto the beach. Shouts rise from the Dragoons, all armed and mounted—no-one is keen to join him—and soon it is clear why. I notice it first— the mare's front hooves sink in further than the hind legs. She throws her head back and whinnies in distress, answered by at least four of the other horses, lined up along the edge of the beach. The sand is moving, liquefying near every movement of her legs, thickening and sinking as if collapsing into a subterranean cave deep below. The terrified horse throws herself on her side, flinging my father from her back at speed—he tumbles, but he is screaming too, leaping to his feet and scrambling away towards us. Behind him, the mare kicks hard to free her front legs from their sandy prison, but she only succeeds in trapping herself further—I can see her wide eyes even from here.

How odd that no-one speaks. Our horses, over forty of them, tread the ground and blow their nostrils; their ears are flat back against their heads. Father roars as he flees, and the mare, encumbered by her saddle, struggles to rise, but rise she must if she is to avoid being sucked under. Father stops. After a second's consideration, he turns and carefully steps back towards the animal, crouching low and calling to her above her panicked whinnying.

'Nooo!' I shout, 'NO! FATHER!' Before I know it, I too have leapt off my own steed and am sprinting down onto the deadly, sandy expanse.

6

With Pistol and Sword

29th February 1792

I reach him in seconds, and together we manage to catch hold of the reins. The poor horse is tired of fighting and paralysed by fear. 'Whoa.' I speak, as lowly and as calmly as I can muster. 'Come on now, come on. Slow, old girl, and steady.' Father's voice stops abruptly—my soothing words are working on man and beast. I pull the reins and gently lean backwards, watching narrowly how far my feet sink into the ground. Tolerably, just a little. I gain courage and pull. Father grasps what I am doing and does the same. Both of us speak quiet encouragement to the horse, and step by step, we pull the mare backwards towards the bank of the beach. Two soldiers have edged forward, stretching for our hands and adding leverage. The horse is exhausted, not to mention covered in sand and shaky-stepped with distress, but she can move her legs well enough. I rub her sand-encrusted withers and use my sleeve to wipe her nostrils clear.

'Come on, old girl, come on. Come with me, girl...' My lilting voice borders on singing, and the adults let me lead the horse away—they crowd around my father, offering him whisky, water, sweet bread and cheese. They slap him on the back and shake his hand. I lead the wheezing mare towards my own stallion and reach into the saddlebags for my waterskin, pour some into my upturned cap and let the poor creature drink. Three more repeats, and the mare seems a little calmer, coughing and swishing her tail. I feel all along her joints to make sure there is no lasting damage. Finally, I press my lips to the waterskin myself and drink the last dregs, feeling my legs wobble. The carronades from the schooner fire once more, as if to say, *'Don't even think about it.'*

But we have to think about it. Worse, we have

to see it through. We are the Excise and they are the smugglers.

'Is she hurt, Henry?' Father has come back up beside me, patting the mare on the hind and running his own skilful hands over her legs, neck and face. I know the man—he loves horses more than he loves people. I'm not surprised he turned back to save her.

'Without you she may have been dead, sir,' I remark.

'Without me,' he answers, 'she wouldn't have been in such peril in the first place.'

He states it as a fact. No apology, no regret, just an honest observation. 'Come now, Henry, we need to determine what to do next.'

Crawford and Burns are in the middle of a council with the Quartermaster.

Crawford glances at me: 'There's nothing for it. Burns and I here were just agreeing that we need to try the boats. The tide is still on the rise, and while the quicksand would probably not be as dangerous for us if we walked, the water would be knee-high at least, and deeper in places.'

The Quartermaster nods and walks over to his

soldiers, pointing at a gaggle of boats upturned a few hundred yards along the coast. They jog towards them as one.

We wait. But they do not return with the boats, nor do they push a single one towards the water as they were instructed. No, they gesture with their hands and one of the men sprints back to us. 'They're all damaged sir,' he gasps between breaths. 'Someone has deliberately holed all the boats.'

The sound Crawford emits is more animal than human. Frustration and anger are etched on Father's face too, but not surprise. Now the tapping and hammering noises of the morning make sense. No-one was repairing boats. They were sabotaging them!

'What could be the motivation for such an act?' Burns asks, but Father is dismissive. 'It's obvious, isn't it? No hay for our horses, no fire in our grates. No help from the locals because they are in league with the smugglers. They set to profit, they do. There will be plenty of wine and tobacco for the smugglers' friends, don't you see? They will never be short of salt or sugar, of candles or rum. The people of these shores would rather ruin their own boats than be of help to us. There's many a Solway man who has thrown his lot in with the smugglers and been richly rewarded. Even the womenfolk are in on it. Rascals all!'

Memories of the conversation I overheard at the inn's window dance through my mind. Old Finlay is such a person. Mary is in on it too, like the rest. I want to spit with disgust. *Wait till I confront them about it, once this schooner is finally apprehended!*

'Then there remains only one way, gentlemen,' Crawford croaks, slinging a rope ladder around his neck. 'Forward on foot, before the tide is too high. Waiting is tantamount to asking her to sail away scot-free without as much as an Excise boot setting foot on her.'

The schooner fires another round of musketry, as if it had overheard.

'Lewars?' Crawford asks, impatience in his voice.

Father sighs and nods. 'But we have to hold our pistols high above our heads.'

'Burns?'

'Yes, Mr Crawford. It seems there is no other way.' The poet's words sound a little strained now, but he still hums, taking his notebook out of his breast pocket and tucking it safely into his saddle bag. I feel a pang of jealousy. He has another life, another calling, beyond any of us.

Crawford looks at us expectantly, but all the men's eyes are on the whirling water, getting higher and higher as the tide comes in. If we don't go soon, it will become impossible. As it is, we may find our escape route cut off. I take off my coat and heavy jerkin, throwing them down on the beach.

'*I'm* ready,' I speak into the silence. I am not staying behind, and I wager, rightly, that Father's thoughts are too occupied to protest.

'Make ready, Dragoons!' shouts Mr Crawford, handing me one of his pistols. 'Are you so feared of the smugglers that this lad is willing, and you are not? Prepare yourselves. We set off immediately, else we lose them! Onwards. I'll take the fore with Lewars, you can take the aft,

Manly, and you Burns, as discussed, go for the broadside. Reserve your fire till within eight yards of the vessel, then fire a volley and board her with pistol and sword.'

The group of soldiers split into three—the first third joins Father and Crawford who lead the way as I tag on at the end. The second marches after the Quartermaster. The poet follows us with the remaining soldiers.

I make it my business to keep close—whatever the Mr Crawford may have said about my courage, I am a full head shorter than the smallest of the men—the tide will wash over me before anyone else, but Father seems to have forgotten about that for now. He is checking his pistol as he walks.

The smugglers on the schooner are obviously watching closely, for as we walk along the beach towards the ever-approaching water's edge, they shoot their carronades once more, making high splashes in the water where the cannonballs fall.

'Don't be feared,' exclaims Burns. 'If we stick to our angles, they can't hit us. They can make a noise, but they can't do damage to body or soul.'

'Well said, Burns!' shouts Crawford at the head of our group and we pick up our pace.

The hazy February sun does little to warm our faces—a clammy chill, rises from the sea, which is calm enough for now. The cold settles on us like a blanket as we approach, and all conversation falls silent. Even the poet has stopped humming. I don't know why, but I had assumed we'd stop for a prayer before entering the water. However, Father and Crawford don't even break their stride, splashing into the surf up to their knees.

I lock my teeth together to stop myself wincing as the blade of icy water cuts my breath off for a moment. Father marches on undaunted, until he checks over his shoulder and his eyes fall on me. A strange expression spreads over his face.

Does he wonder if he is leading his son and heir to his death?

Chapter 7

Of Quill & Ink

29th February 1792

The men are looking to Father, no doubt wondering why he has stopped.

'Onwards,' he croaks, biting his lip to stop his teeth chattering.

Each step is slow and slovenly. We battle against the swirling underwater sand, the seabed which shifts with every step. Water engulfs our boots and rubs our sandy breeches against our prickling skin.

'Keep moving!' shouts Crawford from the front, as wintry waves unbalance us.

I inhale deeply and mechanically, grateful for every breath. The water is up to the men's waists, but up to *my* chest. I struggle to keep my balance, and my pistol is hit by so many sprays of water that I doubt it'll fire at all, even if I needed it to. My arms ache from holding it overhead and even though I know how to work the weapon, I have never been trusted to shoot one before. That thought constrains my throat a little.

The soldier in front of me stumbles sideways at a cannonball crashing into the water, much too close for comfort. The fire from the ship changes to pistols, but we are still too far away.

'They're adjusting their carronades!' yells Quartermaster Manly. 'Swiftly now and bear right! We are nearly upon them!'

A huge splash to my left actually knocks me off my feet, and my pistol is washed away in the waves. I was half-expecting it, so I am back on my feet fast—the soldier in front is not so lucky. I reach forward, spreading my legs wide to steady myself as I pull him upwards. His eyes are scrunched shut when he comes up for air.

'Hold on to each other's scabbards. Pistols over your heads!' shouts Father. Burns's group splits off from ours, making for the broadside of the looming vessel. The gunfire ceases from the ship as the sailors disappear from view.

'They're abandoning ship!' yells Crawford. 'Quickly now! They are destroying the cargo!'

The water is up to my shoulders, but we are very near the ship now. There is no sign of movement on deck anymore, not that I can see.

The next thing I know, a rope is uncoiling in the air above us: Crawford has thrown the rope ladder which easily hooks onto the side of the ship. He is upon it in a heartbeat, sword in hand. More ropes fly and we follow.

The wind is painful as we emerge from the seas; it's as if I had gathered three times my bodyweight and it takes all of my strength to pull myself free from the icy brine. Each step up is more cumbersome than the last, even though Father holds the rope ladder for me and pushes me upwards.

There isn't a single smuggler left on the boat. I see them all in the distance, but to my mind, they are not so much villains now, but God's desperate creatures, swimming and thrashing across the Solway Firth towards England on the southern horizon. I'm only glad that they ran out of time to float their lifeboat. At least we won't have to wade back to land in the same manner that we arrived.

'Contraband!' Crawford puffs, looking around for loot. 'This'll only be the half of it. They're bound to have thrown much of it overboard in their haste.'

I sink to my knees while those soldiers who still have dry gunpowder send salves of bullets after the fleeing smugglers.

'Too far away! They will surely reach England, where we can't get to them, and that shore has dry sand for a long way!' grumbles Crawford and puts his pistol away. 'These rogues will live to thieve another day!'

It takes a while for him to loosen his features after that, but Mr Crawford has reason to smile, and gradually, Father and Burns relax, too. After all, the ship is seized and made safe. We have succeeded.

'*The Rosamund*,' Father muses as he flicks through the papers on the brig. 'That's what this ship is called. It says here that she's a Plymouth vessel. We'll need to auction her and the goods at Dumfries. Henry, don't dither. Make yourself useful!'

And despite the seawater dripping from my clothes with every step, I fetch a sheet of clean paper and ink from the lower deck and begin to make an inventory. I read and write better than most of the soldiers, of that I'm sure.

'Your hand is steady,' the poet observes over my shoulder. 'And you know the words.'

'I like the quill and ink.' I embellish the last line I have written a little as I answer, so he'll think well of me, if I'm honest. Father would never approve of such vanity.

The poet leans forward and lowers his voice.

'Mind what I say: quill and ink are more powerful than all the musket balls and all the cannon in the world put together.' He winks, but something has caught his eye: the carronades, all lined up along the deck, ready to be taken to Dumfries for auction. He chuckles to himself.

I do not attend the auction in Dumfries some weeks after, and the smuggling coast has gone quiet for a bit, so Mr Crawford says. Twice in those days, I pass Mary on the road, riding Old Finlay's donkey. *Is she passing on smuggling news, right under my nose?*

It took me a few days to think it over, but I've resolved not to say anything about the old man and the girl. Men like Crawford may be brave, but a lassie riding all night along the coast to protect her grandfather, that's a different kind of courage. If Old Finlay was offered payment to keep us out of the schooner's way, he had little choice. He has to eat. *The life we have been given…*

By the dim candlelight (and the wailing of my younger siblings, confined to their bedchamber for the evening) I struggle with my numbers, with reckoning-weights and law books. If I am to make an Exciseman one day, I must know these things. I must be good with numbers, not merely with words. Sighing, I glance behind me and check.

Good, Mother has left the room to tend the fires upstairs. The sun has set and Father will be home soon, but I'll hear the hoofbeats.

Feeling guilty and exhilarated at the same time, I slide aside my calculations to reveal a tiny book, bound in red leather and encasing a tight wad of pages.

'I found this in the ship's captain's quarters,' the poet had said to me on the schooner that day in February. 'Would you like it?'

At the time, I looked over my shoulder to check, but Father was overseeing the retrieving of tea chests from below deck.

'For me?'

'Yes, for you. This is the life we have been given, and we must make the best of it. Anyone who loves quill and ink deserves something to use them on. That goes for men and boys.'

The poet tapped my shoulder, a fleeting smile already twinkling away as he turned his attention back to the inventory, and I tucked the book gratefully into my pocket.

And here, by the soft light of the tallow candle, with screaming babes above stairs and me below,

I haltingly compose my first verse.

Down by the coast, black water swirls and hides its secrets.

But for now, I care not.

The End

Glossary

Breeches—trousers

Carronade—short, cast-iron cannon

Contraband—smuggled or stolen goods

Criffel—a distinctive hill, dominating the landscape west of Dumfries

Dominie—a teacher or tutor

Dram—a measure of whisky

Dragoon—a soldier who moved on horseback, but dismounted to fight

Excise—government department for tax on goods

Excise Officer/Exciseman—a government official in the Excise

Free-traders—this is what smugglers used to call themselves

Gauging stick—a measuring tool used by the Excise

Musket—a muzzle-loaded long gun, a firearm

Quaich— a shallow two-handled drinking cup or bowl. From Gaelic 'cuach' meaning 'cup'

*Riding Officer—*an Excise official who patrolled the coast

*Scabbard—*a sheath for the blade of a sword or dagger

*Schooner—*a large sailing ship with two or more masts

*Shearwater—*a long-winged seabird

*Short telescope—*named after James Short, astronomer and telescope maker in the 18th-century

Author's Note

I doubt na, whyles, but thou may thieve;
What then? poor beastie, thou maun live!
(Robert Burns, from *To a Mouse*)

The mouse in the poem may be thieving, but it's got to live, hasn't it? Maybe Burns saw the smugglers and their friends in a similar light.

In 2015, I entered a writing contest—called the Ballantrae Smugglers' Story competition. The challenge was to write a smuggler's story set in the 18th century, ideally located around Ballantrae. I set to work and, immediately, the character of Henry came to mind—a boy reluctantly following his father's footsteps in the Excise. It was an unusual perspective, because as far as I can tell, all the romanticism has been hogged by the smugglers!

I won, and the judge's comments planted a seed. 'This reads almost like the opening chapter of a novel'.

Years later, I had a lightbulb moment. Burns

worked as an Exciseman, did he not? Could he feature in this world? Could I weave the bard into my bairn's tale?

I began to research the Excise years of Burns' life with enthusiasm and found what can only be described as a gift: the incident with the stranded schooner *Rosamund*. Here was a real-life event where I know the poet to have been present, in his role as an Exciseman. Here was a blow-by-blow account kept by the conscientious Riding Officer Walter Crawford and it had everything. EVERYTHING! Desperate smugglers, cannon fire, horses, Dragoons, a race against the tide, illicit activity, corrupt locals, pistols, contraband. For goodness sake, it even had quicksand! All I had to do was to relocate the original idea to Dumfries- and Annanshire and throw my young apprentice into the fray. The father-son dynamic which had been so central to the short story actually worked better in the pressure cooker of the *Rosamund* stranding where every tactical decision could spell failure or even death.

As with all historical fiction, I tend to work best when I have visited the settings and places, watching the waves crash onto the very rocks I describe in my story. I cunningly contrived a reason to spend a family holiday near Dumfries and dragged my family straight from a family wedding in Glasgow to rural Dumfries-shire. There I spent my days typing on beaches and staring at the endless mirror-stretch of the Solway Firth, seeing smuggling schooners in my mind.

I finished *Black Water* there, and I genuinely hope that you love immersing yourself in its world as much as I have.

Smuggling in Scotland and the Real Seizure of the Rosamund

Smuggling in Scotland is the stuff of stories and legend, and from the evidence available, it is almost certain that the majority of goods brought into Scotland illegally were landed on the northern shore of the Solway Firth. It was relatively close to Ireland and the unregulated Isle of Man from where the crossing to Scotland was less than 30 miles.

Southwest Scotland saw an opportunity, and local sailors often worked together to outwit the Excise Officers whose job it was to ensure that everyone paid the right tax on imported goods such as spirits, tea, salt, candles and tobacco. The process worked the other way too—illegally distilled whisky from Scotland was often smuggled to England and beyond.

The famous writer Sir Walter Scott wrote: *"Few People take more enthusiastically to the 'free trade' than the men of the Solway Coast"* and there is no doubt that the smuggling fraternity was often admired for their daring deeds. Even respected members of the local community got involved in smuggling or turned a blind eye to illicit night-time activities on their shores. In general, the people of the area felt that the charges and high taxes were unfair and that the overly-strict rules were made to be broken. Carsethorn and Annan in particular were notorious smuggling hotspots.

To combat these crimes, local men were appointed as Tidesmen, watching out for suspicious vessels. In addition, Riding Officers patrolled the coast almost constantly, with each given a particular stretch of shoreline to monitor. Walter Crawford, the Riding Officer for the Excise, is in charge of the operation described in *Black Water*. Incredibly, his detailed diary of the seizure of the *Rosamund* survives.

Robert Burns was appointed to the Excise in 1791 and promoted to the Dumfries Port Division in February 1792. Not long afterwards, alongside his colleague John Lewars, he took part in the seizure of the *Rosamund*.

Extracts from Crawford's Journal

February 1792: Dumfries Collection, Dumfries District

Here are a few snippets from the records kept by Walter Crawford during the tense days of February 1792. If you look carefully, you will recognise some of his phrases in the conversations in *Black Water*.

'I set off with Mr Lewars directly.'

'And About noon rode down to the shore where I was informed that the vessel could not get off for want of water. I made an attempt to board her with the military, but when we offered to approach her they hailed us that they would fire on us, if we approached any farther.

As my party had only pistols and were but few in number and a great number of men appearing to be on deck, I stopped the soldiery and [...] asked liberty to come on board, which, after some altercation, they granted.

I boarded her and found twenty-four men

under arms with fifteen rounds of shot each.'

'I returned to shore and, consulting with the officers and military, we agreed that greater force would be absolutely necessary.'

'On the 29th, we approached with Dragoons, […] in all forty four fully accoutered and on horseback. The vessel having fallen down the Solway Firth about a mile from where she was yesterday, and being about a mile within sea mark, most of which space being covered with water and a very heavy current running between us and the vessel, we deemed it impossible to get at her, either on foot or on horseback, so we agreed to search the coast for boats in which to board her.

But the country people, guessing our design, got the start of us and staved every boat on the Coast before we could reach them; the vessel in the mean time keeping up a fire of grape shot and musketry, we resolved as [a] last resource to attempt the passage on foot, as the quick sands made the riding on horseback dangerous, or rather impossible.'

'We drew up the Military in three divisions, determined to approach her and attack her if the stream was fordable, one part fore and aft, and the third on her broadside, the first party being commanded by Quarter Master Manly, the second by myself, and the third by Mr Burns.'

'Our orders to the Military were to reserve their fire till within eight yards of the vessel, then to pour a volley and board her with sword and pistol. The vessel kept on firing, though without any damage to us, as from the situation of the ship, they could not bring their great guns to bear on us, we in the meantime wading breast high and, in justice to the party under my command, I must say with great alacrity.'

'By the time we were within one hundred yards of the vessel, the crew gave up the cause, got over [the] side towards England, which shore was for a long, long way dry sand.

As I still supposed that there were only country people they were putting ashore, and that the crew was keeping under cover to make a more vigorous immediate resistance, we marched up as first concerted, but found the vessel completely evacuated both of crew and every moveable on board, expect as per inventory, the smugglers as their last instance of vengeance having poured a *six-pounder Carronade through her broadside. She proved to be the Rosamond of Plymouth.'*

Let's finish on a couple of interesting facts:

1. Historical records often vary in spelling. The Riding officer is referred to as 'Crawford' and 'Crawfurd', while the ship is called both 'Rosamond' and 'Rosamund'. In *Black Water*, we have chosen a spelling and stuck with it.

2. According to some records, Burns purchased four of the carronades of the schooner and sent them to the revolutionaries in France as a mark of his admiration. However, the weapons were apprehended at Dover.

The Poetry of Robert Burns

There are two Burns songs featured in *Black Water*. To ease the tense atmosphere at the inn in Gretna, the poet sings 'The Gallant Weaver', a lesser-known Burns song about marrying for love and not for money. 'The Gallant Weaver' was published in James Johnson's *Scots Musical Museum* in 1792, the same year that the seizure of the *Rosamund* took place. Burns's reference to the River Cart places the tale in the weaving town of Paisley where a thriving textile industry sprung up around then. You can read more about that in *A Pattern of Secrets*, Lindsay Littleson's novel set in Victorian Paisley.

The Gallant Weaver
Where Cart rins rowin to the sea,
By mony a flower and spreading tree,
There lives a lad, the lad for me,
He is a gallant Weaver.

Oh I had wooers aught or nine,
They gied me rings and ribbans fine;

And I was fear'd my heart wad tine
And I gied it to the Weaver.

My daddie sign'd my tocher-band
To gie the lad that has the land,
But to my heart I'll add my hand
And give it to the Weaver.

While birds rejoice in leafy bowers,
While bees delight in opening flowers,
While corn grows green in simmer showers,
I love my gallant Weaver.

The second song could easily have been inspired by the poet's day job as an Excise Officer, although the lyrics seem to imply that Excisemen, who collected taxes and chased smugglers, were bad people who deserved to be taken away by the devil. If that happened, everyone would be so happy they would dance!

Perhaps this shows that Burns had some sympathy with the ordinary people who resorted to smuggling, and that he didn't take himself too seriously!

The Deil's awa wi' the Exciseman

The deil cam fiddlin' thro' the town,

And danc'd awa wi' th' Exciseman;

And ilka wife cries, Auld Mahoun,

I wish you luck o' the prize, man.

The deil's awa the deil's awa,

The deil's awa wi' the Exciseman,

He's danc'd awa he's danc'd awa

He's danc'd awa wi' the Exciseman.

We'll mak our maut, and we'll brew our drink,

We'll laugh, sing, and rejoice, man;

And mony braw thanks to the meikle black
deil,

That danc'd awa wi' th' Exciseman.

The deil's awa the deil's awa,

The deil's awa wi' the Exciseman,

He's danc'd awa he's danc'd awa

He's danc'd awa wi' the Exciseman.

There's threesome reels, there's foursome reels,

There's hornpipes and strathspeys, man,

But the ae best dance ere came to the Land

Was, the deil's awa wi' the Exciseman.

The deil's awa the deil's awa ,

The deil's awa wi' the Exciseman,

He's danc'd awa he's danc'd awa

He's danc'd awa wi' the Exciseman.

Robert Burns

Acknowledgements

Thanks to

Anne Glennie and Kelly Macdonald of Cranachan for being my illicit companions on this journey through the night, and for smuggling *Black Water* into the hands of risk-ready readers.

To Sandra McGowan for putting her quill to paper for the lovely drawings.

The University of Edinburgh's Scottish Literature Department, the Writers Museum in Edinburgh and the Ballantrae Smugglers' Festival who all played their covert parts in sneaking this story into being.

Frances Wilkins, author of *Annandale's Smuggling Story*, for being my secret informer in all questions of authenticity. No-one knows more about the Solway Firth and its smuggling history than her!

My ever-patient family who tolerate my clandestine research ruses, despite the fact that I dragged them to drenched Dumfries-shire during the muddiest, wettest spring on record.

Sorry. I know you still love me, right?

And to my NessBookFest mob, my SCBWI squad, my church gang and my crew of companions on this choppy black water of life, THANK YOU! I am so grateful to God for you all.

About the Author

Barbara Henderson is the author of the historical novels *Fir for Luck* and *Punch*, and of the eco-thriller *Wilderness Wars*. She is a columnist for a range of newspapers in the North of Scotland and lives in Inverness with her family.

She is well-known for her lively school visits and, as a drama teacher, loves to get young readers on their feet.

Find out more about Barbara at www. barbarahenderson.co.uk, and connect with her on Twitter and Instagram (@scattyscribbler) and on Facebook (/barbarahendersonwriter).

Barbara, working on *Black Water* by the shore of the Solway Firth

Also by Barbara Henderson

Fir for Luck

Punch

Wilderness Wars